The Goof Who Invented Homework

and Other School Poems

by **Kalli Dakos**

illustrated by **Denise Brunkus**

Dial Books for Young Readers New York

Published by Dial Books for Young Readers
A member of Penguin Putnam Inc.
375 Hudson Street
New York, New York 10014

Designed by Amelia Lau Carling
Printed in China
First Edition
10 9 8 7

Library of Congress Cataloging in Publication Data
Dakos, Kalli.
The goof who invented homework, and other school poems / by Kalli Dakos ;
illustrated by Denise Brunkus.—1st ed.   p.   cm.
Summary: A collection of poems that reflect the varied, sometimes
funny, sometimes serious activities and emotions of the school year.
ISBN 0-8037-1927-2 (trade).—ISBN 0-8037-1928-0 (lib. bdg.)
1. Schools—Juvenile poetry.   2. Education—Juvenile poetry.
3. Children's poetry, American.   [1. Schools—Poetry.
2. American poetry.]   I. Brunkus, Denise, ill.   II. Title.
PS3554.A414G66 1996 811'.54—dc20 95-38294 CIP AC

To my sisters,

Kathy, Alexandra, and Kristine,

for all the poetry we've shared,

and to Nanette Kane,

the guardian angel of these poems

K.D.

Contents

Have a Great School Year

"My goodness! My goodness!"
Cried the desk.
"It's already the day before school starts,
  And the end of our peace and quiet."

"Ouch," yelled the pencils.
"We'll be heading
  Into those sharpeners soon."

"Oh, me! Oh, my!" sighed the stapler,
  Lying in a pool of sunshine.
"It can't be the end
  Of another summer already!"

"It sure is," laughed the golden leaf,
  Peering in the window.
"Don't you like my
  Gorgeous new outfit?
  I think I look
  Simply marvelous!"

"Just don't get too beautiful,"
  Warned the textbook,
"Or some student
  Will grab you off the tree,
  And stick you inside a book,
  And keep you there forever.
  Why, I once knew a leaf
  Who was stuck inside a book
  For twenty-two years.
  He said he memorized
  Every word and letter
  On the page."

"If anyone's interested
  In my opinion,"
  Interrupted the blank paper,
"I can hardly wait
  Until the kids come back.
  Do you think it is fun to be
  Blank,
  Blank,
  Blank?
  I can't wait until someone
  Writes on me."

"I hope they *won't* write on me,
  Because it can hurt,"
  Moaned the desk.

"Last year Gary wrote,

> *Roses are red,*
> *Violets are blue,*
> *I'm in love*
> *With Jenny Lou.*

Then he got in a fight
With Jenny and changed
The word 'love' to 'hate.'
Was that painful!"

"I can't wait until
The kids get here,"
Giggled the comic book.
"They love me
And always take me
From the classroom library first."

"You're lucky,"
Said the purple book.
"I've been on the shelf
For two years now,
And no one has read me."

"That's because you're
Boring,
Boring,
Boring,"
Added the bulletin board.

"It's not my fault,"
  Cried the book.
"*I* didn't write me."

"I can't see anything!"
  Complained the wad of gum.
"Someone stuck me
  Under this desk
  Five years ago,
  And I'm still here."

"I know how you feel,"
  Sighed the crumpled paper.
"I've been trapped
  In the garbage bucket
  Since the last day of school.
  I just hope I get recycled."

"Wow!"
  Said the brand-new ruler.
"I'm glad I was picked
  To go to a school,
  Instead of some dull old office."

"I hear someone
  Coming down the hall,"
  Screeched the door.
"Everyone, be quiet!"

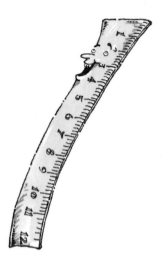

"It's just the custodian,
 With the recycling bin,"
He said a few moments later.

"Oh, oh!"
 Said the crumpled paper,
"I'm out of here!"

They all held their breaths
As the custodian came
Into the room
And emptied the garbage.

"Say hi to the kids
And Mrs. Joseph for me,"
Called the crumpled paper
As he went out the door.

"And have a great school year!"

Ms. Smackaroo

They call her Ms. Smackaroo—
If you're naughty, she kisses you!

In this class, be good as gold,
Do precisely what you're told,

Mark my words, for they are true . . .
Or you'll get a Smackaroo!

Announcements

Your attention, please. . . .

For lunch today there is soup and grilled cheese,
Hamburgers, salad, and five thousand peas.

The door to the boys' room is stuck again,
Will someone let out the custodian?

The ceiling is leaking in class twenty-two,
We're sending umbrellas up to you.

A bag in the office is starting to squirm,
If you are the owner, please come get your worms.

A rooster is lost in the school today,
Oops! I forgot. The third-grade play . . .

Will be in the theatre at quarter past three,
We need the principal—where can she be?

She's chasing the rooster down the hall,
Please come to the office, Mrs. Rawl!

There's Nothing Special in My Bag, Except

Emily: There's something in Jim's book bag,
It's moving all about,
There's something in Jim's book bag,
And it's trying to get out.

Teacher: Just a moment, Emily,
Now pay attention, Bart,
Put away your spelling words,
It's time to work on art.

Jim, please check your book bag,
And tell me what's inside.
I hope there's nothing in there
That you are trying to hide.

Jim: *I have crayons and a pen and two comic
books from Ben. There's my homework
crumpled up and my brand-new little pup
there beside my running shoe and my
leaking tube of glue. There's nothing special
in my bag, except a little tail that wags
and a roll of glitzy tape for my purple
dragon cape.*

Teacher: Thanks for the list, Jim,
Lauren, stop that fight,
Nick, your giant beetle
Is quite an awesome sight.

Emily: There's something in Jim's book bag,
It's *still* moving all about,
There's something in Jim's book bag,
And it's trying to get out.

Teacher: Emily, stop fretting,
Jim says he just has—

Puppy: Woof! Woof!
Woof! Woof!

Teacher: What's that?
I hear a . . . dog.

Puppy: Woof! Woof!
Woof! Woof!

Teacher: Why does your book bag bark and sway,
What *did* you bring to school today?

Jim: No one was listening when I said
I brought my pup. His name is Ned.

A Few Words From Your Test

What am I?

A razor-sharp hatchet,
Ready to chop
Off your head
With one blow,
And serve it
On a silver platter
To your teacher
. . . and parents.

Four Wishes

I made four wishes
On the day
My fifth-grade teacher
Took us on a field trip
To the top of a mountain.

As the school bus
Left the city,
It drove past
Rows of shops,
Miles of concrete,
And acres
Of apartment buildings . . .

Until,
Like a fading dream,
The city was left behind.

My window was dirty,
So I rubbed it
With a tissue
And then squished my nose
Against it
So I could see.

Someone planted
A zillion trees
Out there,
And I wanted to pick
The one that was so bushy
It could hide me,
Like a secret,
Inside its branches.

That's when I made
My first wish.
I wished I could
Take home that tree
And plant it outside
My classroom window,
So I could rest
In its branches
At recess,

And sometimes
I could climb to the top
And look
Through the smog,
To see if the sun
Was still there.

Then I saw the flowers!
Two zillion, in colors
I had never seen before,
And right away,
I changed my wish.

Instead of one tree,
I wished
I could bring back
A field of flowers,
To run in at lunchtime.

But then I saw the river
And it was deeper
Than any blue
I had ever seen,
And I knew
That in all my collection
Of seventy-eight crayons
There wasn't a single one
That could color this river.
So I had to change my wish,
Again.

I wished
I could bring back
An entire river
And place it beside my school.
When someone called me
A bad name,
Or when I failed
A spelling test,
I'd go and sit beside
The water
And let my troubles
Trickle over the rocks,
Splash over the waterfalls,
And flow out to the sea.

But then we rode a gondola
To the top of the world
Where it was so quiet
That I could hear
The winds whispering,
And one bird,
Singing to an audience
Of mountain peaks
Sprinkled with snow
Like sugar.

I sat on a rock,
And watched
A baby squirrel
Come out and look at me,
As if he wondered
What I was doing
On his rocky peak.

He left me imagining
What it would be like
To live
As his brother
On this mountain.

Then, I made
My last and final wish.
I wished
I could bring back
The whole mountain,
And place my school
At the very top
With the squirrels,
And the whispering winds,
And the frosted mountain peaks.

Every day,
I'd ride a gondola
To my school
At the top of the world.

Of course,
These were only wishes,
And all too soon,
We had to ride back down again.
And board the bus,
And pass the river,
And the flowers,
And the trees,
And soon we were
Home again,
In our concrete world.

But sometimes,
When I sit at my desk
At school,
And close my eyes
A certain way,
I can see
The mountain peaks
And the flowers and trees,
And I can hear
The winds and the river
Rushing on to the ocean.

Then I know
That I have
All of that beauty
Inside of me,
And that
As long as I do,
All of my wishes
Have come true.

The Teacher's Head

Teacher: Tom, where's your head this morning?

Tom: I think that I forgot my head.
I must have left it home in bed.
There is a quiz I have to take,
I need a head that's wide-awake.

Ben: I cannot spell; I cannot write,
My cursive is a ghastly sight.
But if you'd like to use my head,
I'll try to borrow Sue's instead.

Sue: A boy with the head of a girl?
It's enough to make *my* head whirl!
But on one condition, it's okay—
I need a head for math today.

Jennie: My brain does math lickety-split,
So help yourself; I'm tired of it.
Use my head, that will be best,
And while you do, I'll take a rest.

Teacher: To loan your head, you are so kind,
But if you want to change your mind,
I could have that rest instead,
And lend you my teacher's head.

Jennie: I do declare! I do declare!
The teacher's head, I'd love to wear,
For with it on, I guarantee,
All the kids will listen to me!

Countdown to Recess

Sun climbs,
Wind chimes.
Five minutes until recess.

A baseball glove,
A game I love.
Four minutes until recess.

I whisper to Pat,
"Get ready to bat."
Three minutes until recess.

My work's all done,
I gotta run.
Two minutes until recess.

Clock, hurry!
Hands, scurry!
One minute until recess.

Brrrrrrrrrrrrrrrrrrrrrrrrrrrring!

Dash!
Gone in a flash!

Twenty Years

Come here!
Come here!
Join the cheers,
For the one
Who spent
Twenty years . . .
          In kindergarten!

          Give us a   T
          Give us an E
          Give us an A
          Give us a   C
          Give us an H
          Give us an E
          Give us an R

What does it spell?
          Teacher.

          Louder!

          TEACHER!

          Yeah!

The Secret

I'll keep your secret
Until I'm ninety-two,
I *won't* tell my friends,
But if somehow I do,
I'll make very certain that
They keep it too!

Murder in the Fourth Grade

I killed Sunny.
I know I did.
Mr. Freeman thinks
It was just a coincidence,
But my best friends,
Kate and Andrew,
Agree with me.

It was murder.

Sunny was my friend
Even though he had fins,
And swam in a fishbowl,
And ate fish food.

I remember the week
I sprained my ankle,
And Mr. Freeman took the kids
For a hike in the park,
And I had to stay behind
In the classroom.
I was so angry,
I thought I'd boil over
Like that substitute teacher did
When all the kids
Glued their math tests
To their desks.

And there was Sunny,
Pressing his nose
Against the fishbowl,
As if he was trying to say,
"I know just how
You feel, Jack,
I'm *always* left out too.
You think it's a pain
Having a sprained ankle?
Well, just try being
A goldfish in fourth grade.
I'm left out of everything."

After that,
Whenever I went by Sunny's bowl,
I imagined him talking to me.

"Hey, Jack,
Fish food tastes like shavings
From the pencil sharpener.
Sure wish I could eat
Some of those candies
You keep sneaking
From your desk."

The rest of the time,
I didn't think of Sunny
All that much.
I mean,
How excited
Can a fourth grader get
Over a goldfish?

But then
I murdered him,
And I remembered
The first week of school
When Mr. Freeman said,
"This little fish is going to test you.
You see,
His very life
Depends on you."

I was the only kid in the class
To fail Sunny
In the most important test of all.

If only the tryouts
For the hockey team
Hadn't been
On the exact same week
I was the monitor
In charge of
Feeding Sunny.

I'm one of those kids
Who should have been born
With skates instead of feet,
And that entire week my brain
Was like a chalkboard
With one word on it—
Hockey.

I forgot . . .
My homework
Three days in a row,
My Band-Aid collection
For health,
My book money,
My project on gorillas,
My Dracula teeth
For the play, and . . .

Sunny.

Monday came and went,
And I forgot to feed him.

Tuesday came and went,
And I forgot to feed him.

Wednesday came and went,
And I forgot to feed him.

On Thursday Kate looked
In the fishbowl and cried,
"Sunny looks half-dead.
He's floating
Like an old leaf
On the pond in fall."

Sunny wasn't half-dead.
He was all-dead,
And I had failed
The most important test
Of all.

Mr. Freeman said
Sunny may have been sick
With a fish virus,
And that is why he died.
He said most fish
Would survive,
Even if they were not fed
For three days.

But Kate and Andrew
Say it was
Third-degree murder.

It wasn't first or second,
Because it was a mistake.
It wasn't as if I decided
To murder Sunny
And just flushed
Him down the toilet
Or anything like that.

I mean I didn't set out
To kill him,
But he's dead,
Just the same.

I *did* become captain
Of the hockey team,
And when I'm zipping
Around that ice rink,
I feel like
An Olympic champion.

But even a champion
Can't bring
A goldfish
Back to life,
And no matter
What anyone says,
I am responsible
For the murder
In the fourth grade.

Our Custodian's a Poet

We all know it,
Our custodian's a poet!

When our class
Did papier-mâché,
He wrote on the board
While he cleaned that day:

> *Mucky mess*
> *Of dust and glue,*
> *Papier-mâché,*
> *I don't like you!*

When the rooster escaped
During show-and-tell,
The whole school heard
The custodian yell:

> *Cock-a-doodle-doo,*
> *Cock-a-doodle-doo,*
> *Wait until I get my hands on*
> *Cock-a-doodle-you!*

When it was Jill's turn
To sweep up the room,
Jill chased Rashad
With the big green broom.

Brooms are for sweeping,
Brooms are for floors,
Not chasing young men
Out of the doors.

When Alice barfed up
Her lemonade,
He flew with a bucket
To second grade.

I'm here to handle
All kinds of distress,
I'm Supercustodian,
King of the mess!

Ooooooooooo

Ooooooooooo,
Ooooooooooo,
I am a ghooost
Of this schoool.
Ooooooooooo,
Ooooooooooo,
I was once a kid toooo!

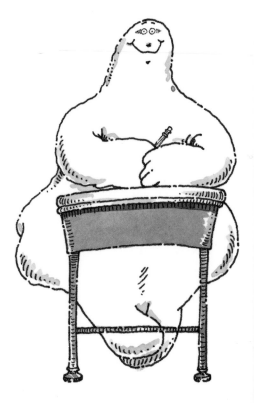

Ooooooooooooo,
Ooooooooooooo,
I'm a stoooodent
From the past.
Ooooooooooooo,
Ooooooooooooo,
I once sat in yoooour class.

Ooooooooooooo,
Ooooooooooooo,
I don't really
Want to booooast.
Ooooooooooooo,
Ooooooooooooo,
But I'm a
Classroooom ghoooost!

I'm the Ghosty

I'm the ghosty,
Who loved school
The mosty!

There's a Bee on My Spelling

Fred: There's a bee on my spelling.

Ms. Hill: There *can't* be a B.
I remember that
You had all the words
Correct,
And I gave you
An A.

Fred: Yes, Ms. Hill,
There's a bee on my spelling,
And I don't know what to do.

Ms. Hill: Check again.
Check again.
It's not a B;
It's an A.

Fred: Ouch! Ouch!
Oooch! Oooch!
IT *IS* A BEE,
AND IT JUST STUNG ME!

Ms. Hill: Well, I'll be.

Cries From the Lunch Box

Sandwich: It's not fair,
It's not fair,
To have cheese
For underwear.

Apple: Would you prefer
To roll around,
Bottoms up,
Stem on the ground?

Raisins: We used to be
Plump juicy grapes,
Now we're dried-up
Wrinkled shapes.

Milk: Four gulps,

Three slurps,

Yum-yum-yum!

Look out,

Stomach,

Here I come!

My Lunch Is Buzzing

My lunch is
    Buzz,
    Buzz,
    Buzzing,

I'm afraid to look inside.

    It's really
    Buzz,
    Buzz,
    Buzzing—

Pass the insecticide!

Back Away! Back Away!

I knew Carol was sick
The first day I met her.

Her skin was as pale
As the sand
That stretches
On the beach
Near my house.

She was so thin,
I was afraid
She would topple over
When the wind blew through
The oak trees
On the playground.

"I have a terrible disease,"
She told me one day,
"But I like to imagine
I'm healthy just like
The other kids."

It was hard to pretend
In our school.

"Back away! Back away!"
Timothy warned his friends,
Whenever she walked
Near them.
"She's covered in germs,
And some of them
Will jump on you."

Whenever this happened,
Her big blue eyes
Turned all watery
As if storm clouds
Were covering the sky,
And she cried,

"My disease is *not* catching."

"We're not taking any chances
That someday we'll
Look like you,"
Some kids would holler,
And then . . .
They'd back away.

"Why?" she would cry.
"Why do they say
 Mean things like that?"

I didn't know the answer,
But whenever she asked,
I felt like crying too.

I liked Carol.
I really liked her.
I think she knew
She was going to die,
But she always
Did her best in school.
She even wanted me
To bring her assignments
When she was home sick.

Why? I wondered.
Why do your schoolwork
If you know you are going to die?

One day I called
To give her
Our spelling words
For the week,
And she answered my question
Without even being asked.

"I love doing my homework,"
 She told me.

"Sometimes when I'm writing a story,
Or studying spelling words,
Or working out math problems,
I forget that I'm sick.
It's like there's a place
Where everyone is healthy,
And even I get to go there . . .
Sometimes."

But even though
She was able to visit that place
Once in a while,
She could never
Stay there because
The mean kids kept yelling,
"Back away! Back away!"

Carol became so sick
That she couldn't
Come to school anymore.

I'd stop at her house
On my way home,
With her homework
Piled on top of my own,
And sometimes
She was so weak,
She could hardly
Hold a pencil
To do her arithmetic.

One sunny winter day
Our class went ice-skating
At the rink near our school,
And when we returned
To the classroom,
The principal told us
That Carol had passed away.

She died while our class—
Her class—
Was having fun
At a skating rink.

I went to her funeral
In my black skirt
And black shoes,
And checked to make sure
The flowers my parents
Had sent were there.

"They can't be red or blue,"
I told my mom.
"They have to be yellow—
Big yellow flowers,
Like the sunshine."

My flowers were there,
And they were the biggest,
Brightest ones
I have ever seen.

Carol's mother came over
While I was looking at them,
And she hugged me so closely,
I could hardly breathe.

Then she whispered,
"Thank you for those
Beautiful flowers,
And for bringing
Carol's homework
So faithfully.
If friendship could be measured
On a report card,
You were an A plus-plus-plus
In her life."

I felt tears
Streaming down my face,
And I ached in places
I had never even
Felt before.

I stood there
For a long time,
Looking at the gigantic petals,
And one tiny seed
Of a thought
Came to me.

Maybe she's there,
I said to myself.

Maybe she's in that place
Where everyone is healthy,
And no one ever yells,

"Back away!
Back away!"

And the thought
Shone as glorious,
And bright,
As those big yellow flowers.

Lucky

Out of all the galaxies
In the universe,
I live in
the Milky Way.

Out of all the planets
In our solar system,
I live on
Planet Earth.

Out of all the teachers
In the world,
I have
Ms. Hogan.

Lucky . . .

Just lucky.

Imaginary Friends

I didn't have a single friend
In my new school—
Not one.

I felt like a crayon
In a box of pencils.

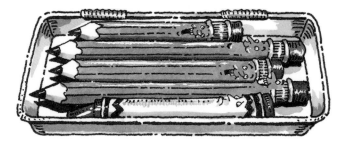

So I made up
Two imaginary friends
Who were just like me—
Jack and Jake.

We played together,
And had a lot of fun
Until we got into a
BIG FIGHT.

Now
Jack and Jake
Play with each other,
But they won't play with

ME!

Thanksgiving

Everyone laughed
At my Band-Aid project
But I'm thankful
I brought it to school,
Because Mr. Zin
Cut his finger
On the paper chopper,
And needed
The biggest bandage of all.

I lost the bag
Of worms
That I've been collecting
For two days,
But I'm thankful
That a first grader
Found it on the playground
And brought it
To the office.

Mary Jane
Tripped on her big toe,
And spilled orange paint
All over my turkey picture,
But I'm thankful
That my favorite color
Is orange—
Even on a turkey.

The kids snickered
At the rock
That I brought to school,
And said
Keenan's rooster
Was a million times
More interesting,
But I'm thankful
That my rock
Didn't escape
During morning announcements
And get me in trouble
With the principal.

Thanksgiving
Is the time
To be thankful
For all the things
That start out wrong,
But somehow end up
Right.

Thank You for the Nots

Thank you, Grayson,
For *not* bringing
Your worm collection
To sharing time.

Thank you, Sarah,
For *not* saying,
"I won't pick up
The coffin bank
Because Garrett
Dropped it on the floor
Before he went home sick."

Thank you, Ryan,
For *not* forgetting
Your pencil with
The spider eraser
Today.

Thank you, Nancy,
For *not* calling
Tyler a beanpole
Just because
Everyone else did.

A special thanks
To all of you
For the *nots*!

Bonkers

This morning
Jason raced
Into our classroom
Screaming,

"Ms. Hogan! Ms. Hogan!
I'm late for school,
And my homework isn't done,
Because I dropped it
On an alligator,
And he ate it all up
In one gulp,
And then wanted to
Eat my feet too,
But I got away!"

Ms. Hogan sighed,
"Jason, you are driving me

Bonk

Bonk

Bonkers!"

After morning recess
Jason tore into the classroom,
Calling,

"Ms. Hogan! Ms. Hogan!
I sat on an anthill
On the playground,
And now there are ants
Running races in my pants
And they are tickling me,
And biting me,
And making me itchy,
And I have to go
To the nurse,
Before they make me
Sick!"

Ms. Hogan sighed,
"Jason, you are driving me

Bonk

Bonk

Bonkers!"

When Jason came back
From the nurse's office,
He yelled,

"Ms. Hogan! Ms. Hogan!
The nurse made me put
Special cream on my rear end
So that the itching would stop,
But if I sit down
The cream will squish
Out of my underwear,
And wreck my pants
And my chair,
So for the rest of the week,
I'll have to do my work
Standing up!"

Ms. Hogan
Took a long look at Jason,
And closed her eyes
As if she wanted to sleep
For a hundred years.

Then she started walking
Across the room,
Chanting,

*"Bonkers! Bonkers!
I'm bonkers at last,
I knew it would happen,
One day in this class!"*

Then the teacher
walked right out the door.

"Ms. Hogan! Ms. Hogan!"
Cried Jason,
"Come back!"

But she kept right on walking.

Jason looked down the hall,
And took a deep breath,
And said,
"Ms. Hogan is the nicest teacher
I've ever had,
And I drove her

Bonk

Bonk

Bonkers!"

A few moments later
Ms. Hogan returned to the classroom,
Carrying a big pile of papers.

Jason was sitting at his desk,
Working quietly.
When he saw Ms. Hogan,
He raised his hand,
And said,

"Ms. Hogan! Ms. Hogan!
I'm so sorry that
I drove you bonkers,
And I hope you don't
Quit being a teacher,
Because you're nice,
And you're fair,
And you helped me to read,
And now I've read
Every book in the classroom,
And I visit bookstores
On the weekends,
And if it wasn't for you,
I'd still feel sick
When my grandma
Or my friends
Gave me a book
For my birthday,
And I promise,
A hundred zillion times,
That I'll never
Drive you bonkers again."

Ms. Hogan smiled.
"You did drive me bonkers, Jason,
But a short walk
Down the hall
Helped me recover.

Besides, there wouldn't be
A single teacher left
On the face of the earth,
If we quit teaching
Just because students
Drove us bonkers."

Jason let out a big sigh
Of relief.

"Ms. Hogan! Ms. Hogan!
You're the best teacher
In the whole wide world,
And I promise
With my heart
And soul
And ears
And eyeballs
That never again
Will I drive you

Bonk

Bonk

Bonkers!"

(But, of course, the next day he did.)

Mr. C's Bad Day

The entire day
Has been:

    Mr. C. THIS,
    Mr. C. THAT,

    Mr. C. COME HERE,
    Mr. C. GO THERE,
    Mr. C. I NEED,
    Mr. C. I WANT,
    Mr. C. I FORGOT,

    Mr. C.,
    Mr. C.,
    Mr. C.

I'm so tired of my name,
Please—
For the rest of the day,
Call me:

MR. D.

The Most Important Time

One day my teacher, Ms. Barber,
Asked us to be reporters.
"Here is your question," she said.
"What is the most important time
In a person's life?"

One team asked the principal,
"Mrs. Rawl, what is the
Most important time
In a person's life?"

Mrs. Rawl rubbed her chin and said,
"That is a very difficult question.
Perhaps it is when one is old
And has great wisdom,
But I can't be sure
If this is the proper answer."

One team asked
The office secretary,
"Ms. Price, what is the
Most important time
In a person's life?"

Ms. Price stopped writing on her
Attendance paper and said,
"That is a very difficult question.
Perhaps it is when one first becomes
A mother or a father,
But I do not know
If this answer is correct."

One team asked Mr. Bergman,
The music teacher,
"What is the most important time
In a person's life?"

Mr. Bergman put down
His trombone and said,
"That is a very difficult question.
I think it is when a person
First learns to love music,
But I am not sure
If this answer is right."

The last team asked
The custodian, Mr. Spiro,
"What is the most important time
In a person's life?"
Mr. Spiro stopped piling boxes
In the storage closet and said,
"That is a very difficult question.
I think it is when you create
Something beautiful,
Like a poem or a painting,
But I am not sure
If this answer
Is the correct one."

We returned to our classroom,
And Ms. Barber asked,
"Did anyone answer your question?"

Each team reported
On the answers
They had received.

Then Melody said,
"Why don't you ask us?
We might know the answer."
"Of course," said Ms. Barber.
"Of course I should ask you."

Then she gave us the question,

"What is the most important time
In a person's life?"

Matthew was so excited,
His hand shot up
Like a rocket,
And before the teacher
Could pick someone to reply,
He yelled,

"That's an easy question!
I know the answer!"

Ms. Barber was surprised.

"You know the answer when
The custodian,
The music teacher,
The secretary,
And the principal did not?"

"Yes! Yes, I do!" screamed Matthew.

"Then what is the most important time
In a person's life?" she asked.

And Matthew replied,
"It's right now, of course,
It's today!
Why, Jessica brought her dancing soda bottle
To school for show-and-tell,
And Terry got his first basket in gym,
And Susie fell out of her chair
Three times in a row,
And there's a bird peeking
In the classroom window
Right this instant,
And he's looking at us
As if he wants to go to school."

We all looked at the bird
For a few moments,
And he looked at us,
And then we grew as quiet
As a school in the summer.

Finally Ms. Barber softly said,
"Thank you, Matthew.
Thank you for answering
Our question."

Sunbeams for a Student

The sky is dark as midnight,
Rain is streaming down out there,
But here inside my classroom,
Sunbeams shimmer everywhere.

A winter storm is brewing
As the rain turns into sleet,
But I can smell the roses,
And I feel the summer's heat.

Leaves cling for life on branches
As winds howl from the west,
But the sun shines all around me,

For I passed my spelling test!

Some Valentine's Day!

Dear Jennifer,
Roses are red,
Violets are blue,
I just decided
I'm in love with you.
Love,
Gary

Gary:

What are you writing
On that piece
Of pink paper?
Work on your test, dummy!
Rick

Rick:

I'm writing
A Valentine's note
To Jennifer.
Brian is so lucky.
He gets to sit beside her.
Tell him to give this
To her.
Gary

Gary:

    I'll give it to Brian
    But I don't like
    The sound of this.
       Rick

         Rick:

            I can't see with Meredith
            In the way.
            Did she get the note?
               Gary

Gary:

    Not yet.
    Brian still has it in his hand.
       Rick

         Rick:

            Why isn't he passing it?
               Gary

Gary:

    Did you forget we're in the
    Middle of a test?
    He's waiting for it to be *all clear.*
    What did you write
    On that valentine anyway?
       Rick

Rick:

I told Jennifer I loved her.

Gary

Gary:

Are you crazy?

You're only eleven years old.

You're too young to be in love!

Rick

Rick:

I realized at lunch

How much I loved her.

She was standing there

Beside the tacos,

When all of a sudden

I felt it—

Love!

Gary

Gary:

Yuck!

Brian just passed the note to her.

I think she's opening it.

Rick

Rick:

What's she doing?

Is she smiling?

Gary

Gary:
> She put her head
> On her desk.
>> *Rick*

      Rick:
>> Is she laughing?
>> Is she crying?
>> I need to know!
>>> *Gary*

Gary:
> Her head is still on her desk.
> The note is still in her hands.
> It looks like she's fallen asleep.
>> *Rick*

      Rick:
>> Asleep?
>> She can't be!
>> Didn't she just find out
>> That I love her?
>>> *Gary*

Gary:
> She's so smart in math,
> She's finished the test
> Already,
> And she's definitely
> Gone to sleep.
>> *Rick*

Rick:

Get Brian to nudge her
And wake her up.
I need to know
If she read the note.
Gary

Gary:

Brian won't.
Rick

Rick:

Tell him I'll lend him
My new hockey stick.
Gary

Gary:

He tried.
She won't wake up.
The note fell
Out of her hand
And now it's on the floor.
Rick

Rick:

Oh, no, no, no!
Tell Brian to get it *fast*!
Gary

Gary:

He wants to *keep* your hockey stick.
Rick

Rick:

    He can have it.

    He can have it.

    Just get that valentine!

        Gary

Gary:

Do I have to remind

You again

That this is a test?

He's waiting for

The right moment!

    Rick

Rick:

    I know!

    I know!

    But what if someone else

    Gets that note?

    Or the teacher?

    Yikes!

        Gary

Gary:

Brian said he'd try,

But he wants

The puck too.

    Rick

Rick:

    He can have the puck.

    And my skates,

    And my computer,

    And my liver

    And kidneys too!

    Just get me that note!

Gary

Gary:

  Brian slithered over

  When Mr. Freeman

  Wasn't looking

  And grabbed the note.

  Now he's reading it!

    Rick

Rick:

    That note is private!

    Get him to STOP!

    Gary

Gary:

  Too late.

  He read it,

  And he won't give it back.

    Rick

Rick:

Tell him he can have
My other hockey stick too!
I want that note!

Gary

Gary:

Jennifer's moving.
She's waking up.
Now she's looking
On the floor
For something.

Rick

Rick:

Do you think
She read it?
I hope not.
I must have been crazy
To send her a love note!
Get it for me!

Gary

Gary:

Brian says he'll give you the note
If you'll play hockey with him
Every day after school.

Rick

Rick:
    I'll buy him
    A skating rink
    If I have to.
    Just get me the note!
        Gary

Gary:
    Brian said to forget the rink.
    Hockey after school
    For the rest of your life
    Is enough.
        Rick

Rick:
    It's a deal.
        Gary

Gary:
    Here's the note.
    Let's hope Jennifer didn't read it.
        Rick

Rick:

    I'm ripping it
    In a zillion pieces.
    You never saw it.
    I never wrote it.
    It never existed.
        Gary

Gary:

  Brian says that as long as
  You play hockey with him,
  He'll forget the note too.
      Rick

Rick:

    I wrote a love note
    To Jennifer
    And I've ended up
    With Brian for the rest
    Of my life!
    Some Valentine's Day!
        Gary

The Book That Made Danny Cry

It is quiet reading time.
Everyone in class is reading,
Except Danny.

He's crying.

I've never seen
Danny cry before—
Not even when
He broke his arm
During recess.

"What's wrong, Danny?"
The teacher asks.

Danny can't talk.
He points to a page
In his book.

"Ah," says the teacher.
"I've read that book too,
And you must be on the
Last chapter."

Danny sniffs and nods.

The teacher pats him
On the head
And says,

"Sometimes good books
Are very sad,
Because life is often sad."

Danny sniffs and nods again.

I sit at my desk
and wonder what book
Danny is reading.

I want to read that book—
The book that made Danny cry!

Mix-ups

Short-Haired Girl in Jeans:
I'm a *she*,
Not a *he*,
So please call me
Stephanie.

Long-Haired Boy in Jeans:
I'm a *he*,
Not a *she*,
So please call me
Gregory.

The Goof Who Invented Homework

Ricky (whispering): What is Mr. Smith
Droning
On and on about?

Sharon (whispering back): Something to do
With a man called
Christopher Columbus.
Wasn't he a cowboy
In the Wild West?

Ricky: No, stupid,
Columbus was
Never a cowboy!
He was one of
Snow White's dwarfs.

Sharon: So who cares?
Cowboy?
Dwarf?
What's the difference?
Now what's the teacher
Rambling on about?

Ricky: He's talking about
Frankenstein.
Isn't he a musician?

Sharon: Yeah,
I think he writes rap music.

Ricky: Me too.
Now he's talking
About another goof
Called Beethoven.
Didn't he invent
The lightbulb?

Sharon: No, stupid.
It wasn't Beethoven!
It was those two brothers,
The Wright Brothers,
I think.

Ricky: I remember now!
It wasn't Beethoven,
But it wasn't the
Wright Brothers either.
They invented
The telephone.
George Washington
Invented the lightbulb.

Sharon: I guess you're right.
George Washington
Was the father
Of the lightbulb.
Now we're doing
Dumb old geography.
Where's Brazil?
It's the capital of England,
Isn't it?

Ricky: No, stupid!
It's not even a capital.
It's a country in China.

Sharon: That's not right.
There's a man from Brazil
On my street
And he doesn't look Chinese.

Ricky: Well, maybe
It's in Texas or India.
Who cares anyway?

Sharon: You've got a point.
Who cares?

Ricky: Oh! Oh!
Did you do
Your math homework?
He's coming to check.
I didn't get that question
On fractions.
If you had a pizza,
And you ate one third of it,
How much would be left?

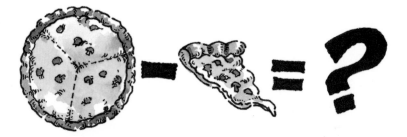

Sharon: Zippo,
Zero,
Absolutely none,
Especially if it had
Pepperoni!

Ricky: You're gonna
Flunk
Flunk
Flunk math.
This is a trick question,
And the answer is that
You'd have one third left.
One third and one third
Equal a whole pizza.

Sharon: So you're brilliant!
Do you wanna medal?

Ricky: No, I just like to have
My brilliance appreciated.
I wonder who the goof was
Who invented homework?

Sharon: I know that one.
It was Alexander Graham Bell.
First he invented the school bell—
Then he invented homework.
Okay, Mr. Brilliant,
I've got one for you.
What is the *Titanic*?
It's a big whale,
Isn't it?

Ricky: No, dummy!
        Not a whale.
        She's the queen
        Of England—
        Queen Titanic.

Sharon: I knew that.
        I really did.
        When is this day gonna end?
        Long,
        Boring,
        Nothing important.
        Who needs school anyway?

I Should Have Studied for this Test

Too many questions
I can't even touch—
Remembering so little,
Forgetting so much.

Tanya's Test

T	erribly
T	ough
T	o
T	ackle
T	oday

T	ake
T	he
T	errifying
T	es-
T	away!

Yahoo, Team Blue!

Yahoo,
Team Blue,
Fight
Fight
Fight!

Go
in
there
and
do
it
right!

Yahoo,
Team Blue,
Win
Win
Win!

Get
the
points
and
bring
them
in!

Yahoo,
Team Blue,
Yes
Yes
Yes!

Win
for
us
this
game
of
chess!

I Lost the Work I Found

Today
I lost
the
work
I found
in
the
lost
and
found
yesterday.

Tomorrow
in
the
lost
and
found
I'll find
the
work
I lost
today
after
I found
it
yesterday.

Homework

I'm a monster
With a giant mouth.
I devour
Your playtime,
And then I burp up
A clock
That says,

"GO TO BED!"

A Good-bye Poem From a Retiring Teacher

For thirty years,
I've watched you grow,
   Run in the sun,
   Play in the snow,
I've watched you grow.

For thirty years,
I've heard your songs,
   Enjoyed the music,
   Sang along,
I've heard your songs.

For thirty years,
I've held your hand,
   Tried my best
   To understand,
I've held your hand.

For thirty years,
I've said good-bye,
   Hoped your wings
   Were strong to fly,
I've said good-bye.

For thirty years,
I played my part,
   Precious memories
   Are in my heart,
I played my part.

For thirty *more* years,
I'll remember you,
   I'll treasure your cards
   And your letters too,
I'll remember you—

For thirty more years!